Phonics Friends

Kella's Kitten
The Sound of K

The Child's World

By Joanne Meier and Cecilia Minden

The Child's World®

Published in the United States of America
by The Child's World®
PO Box 326
Chanhassen, MN 55317-0326
800-599-READ
www.childsworld.com

A special thank you to the Scipes Family and to Julie
Sokolski for graciously allowing us to photograph one
of her gentle Ragdoll kittens.

The Child's World®: Mary Berendes, Publishing Director

Editorial Directions, Inc.: E. Russell Primm, Editorial
Director and Project Editor; Katie Marsico, Associate
Editor; Judith Shiffer, Associate Editor and School Media
Specialist; Linda S. Koutris, Photo Researcher and
Selector

The Design Lab: Kathleen Petelinsek, Design and Page
Production

Photographs ©: Photo setting and photography by Romie
and Alice Flanagan/Flanagan Publishing Services

Library of Congress Cataloging-in-Publication Data
Meier, Joanne D.
  Kella's kitten : the sound of K / by Joanne Meier and
Cecilia Minden.
    p. cm. — (Phonics friends)
  Summary: Simple text featuring the sound of the
consonant "k" describes Kella's new kitten, Kippy.
  ISBN 1-59296-298-X (library bound : alk. paper)
  [1. English language—Phonetics. 2. Reading.] I. Minden,
Cecilia. II. Title. III. Series.
  PZ7.M5148Ke 2004
  [E]—dc22   004002199

Note to parents and educators:

The Child's World® has created Phonics Friends with the goal of exposing children to engaging stories and pictures that assist in phonics development. The books in the series will help children learn the relationships between the letters of written language and the individual sounds of spoken language. This contact helps children learn to use these relationships to read and write words.

The books in this series follow a similar format. An introductory page, to be read by an adult, introduces the child to the phonics feature, or sound, that will be highlighted in the book. Read this page to the child, stressing the phonic feature. Help the student learn how to form the sound with her mouth. The Phonics Friends story and engaging photographs follow the introduction. At the end of the story, word lists categorize the feature words into their phonic element. Additional information on using these lists is on The Child's World® Web site listed at the top of this page.

Each book in this series has been carefully written to meet specific readability requirements. Close attention has been paid to elements such as word count, sentence length, and vocabulary. Readability formulas measure the ease with which the text can be read and understood. Each Phonics Friends book has been analyzed using the Spache readability formula. For more information on this formula, as well as the levels for each of the books in this series please visit The Child's World® Web site.

Reading research suggests that systematic phonics instruction can greatly improve students' word recognition, spelling, and comprehension skills. The Phonics Friends series assists in the teaching of phonics by providing students with important opportunities to apply their knowledge of phonics as they read words, sentences, and text.

This is the letter *k*.

In this book, you will read words that have the *k* sound as in:

kitten, keep, milk, and *like.*

Kella is a lucky girl.

She has a new kitten.

The kitten's name is Kippy.

The kitten is very soft.

Kella's job is to keep

the kitten safe.

Kippy likes to sleep in a basket.

It is a warm place.

Kippy likes to drink milk.

Sometimes Kippy drinks

Kella's milk!

Kippy likes to look out the window. He likes to see the birds.

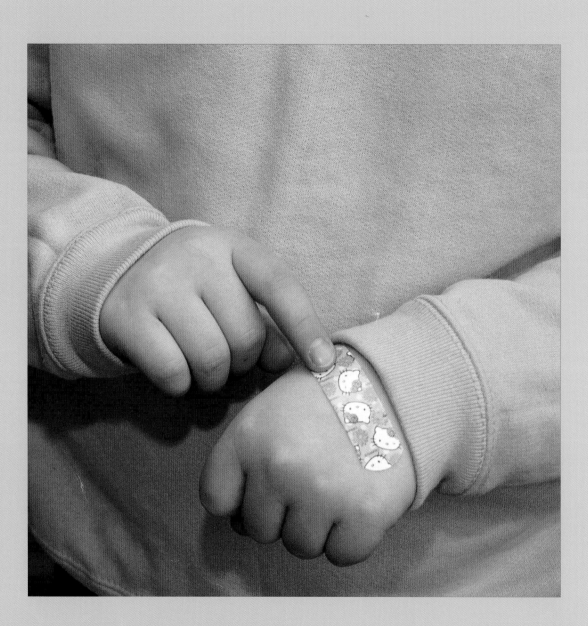

Kella likes to pet Kippy.

Sometimes Kippy scratches.

Ouch!

Kippy sleeps on Kella's bed.

He likes to be warm.

Kella has a new kitten.

Do you have any pets?

Fun Facts

More than 35,000 kittens are born in the United States every day! Most cats give birth to between one and eight kittens at a time. One cat in Texas was the mother of more than 420 kittens! Mother cats often carry kittens around by the scruff of their necks. Just like the eyes of a human baby, a kitten's eyes may change color as it grows older.

Do you like ice cream? Did you know that it takes 10 gallons (38 liters) of milk to make 1 gallon (3.8 L) of ice cream? A dairy cow can produce up to 90 glasses of milk each day and 200,000 glasses of milk in its lifetime! But cows aren't our only source of milk—some farmers also rely on water buffalo, camels, goats, sheep, reindeer, and horses.

Activity

Learning about a Dairy Farm

Are you curious about how milk gets from a cow to your kitchen table? If you want to see firsthand, talk to your parents about contacting a dairy farm in your area. Perhaps you can tour the farm, or possibly speak to one of the workers there. Your can also visit your local library to check out books that explain this process.

To Learn More

Books
About the Sound of K
Flanagan, Alice K. *Kids: The Sound of K*. Chanhassen, Minn.: The Child's World, 2000.

About Kittens
Day, Nancy Raines, and Anne Mortimer (illustrator). *A Kitten's Year*. New York: HarperCollins, 2000.

Ryder, Joanne, and Susan Winter (illustrator). *Come Along, Kitten!*. New York: Simon & Schuster Books for Young Readers, 2003.

Tides, Phyllis Limbacher. *Calico's Curious Kittens*. Watertown, Mass.: Charlesbridge Publishing, 2003.

About Milk
Llewellyn, Claire. *Milk*. New York: Children's Press, 1998.

Powell, Jillian. *Milk*. Austin, Tex.: Raintree/Steck-Vaughn, 1997.

Taus-Bolstad, Stacy. *From Grass to Milk*. Minneapolis: Lerner Publications, 2004.

Web Sites
Visit our home page for lots of links about the Sound of K:
http://www.childsworld.com/links.html

Note to Parents, Teachers, and Librarians: We routinely check our Web links to make sure they're safe, active sites—so encourage your readers to check them out!

K Feature Words

Proper Names
Kella
Kippy

Feature Words in Initial Position
keep
kitten

Feature Words in Medial Position
basket
like
lucky

Feature Words in Final Position
drink
look
milk

About the Authors

Joanne Meier, PhD, has worked as an elementary school teacher and university professor. She earned her BA in early childhood education from the University of South Carolina, and her MEd and PhD in education from the University of Virginia. She currently works as a literacy consultant for schools and private organizations. Joanne Meier lives with her husband Eric, and spends most of her time chasing her two daughters, Kella and Erin, and her two cats, Sam and Gilly, in Charlottesville, Virginia.

Cecilia Minden, PhD, directs the Language and Literacy Program at the Harvard Graduate School of Education. She is a reading specialist with classroom and administrative experience in grades K–12. She earned her PhD in reading education from the University of Virginia. Cecilia and her husband Dave Cupp enjoy sharing their love of reading with their granddaughter Chelsea.